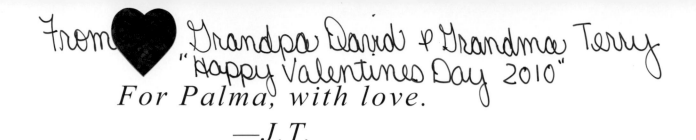

To: Hannah From ♥ Grandpa David & Grandma Terry
"Happy Valentines Day 2010"

For Palma, with love.
—J.T.

Barnes & Noble
122 Fifth Avenue
New York, NY 10011

ISBN-13: 978-1-4351-2376-2

Produced by Fun Union
Printed and bound in China
1 3 5 7 9 10 8 6 4 2

The Legend of Lyla the Lovesick Ladybug

Written by Joe Troiano

Illustrated by Susan Banta

Holiday Hill Farm®
holidayhillfarm.com

Lyla the Ladybug
lived in a rose,
in the Holiday Hill greenhouse,
where row
after row
of roses grow.

Those roses were growing for Valentine's Day,
so people in love could give them away.

Lyla thought about love.
She thought about it a lot.
She wondered…
what made someone love you,
or…love you not.

Hour after hour,
Lyla cared for her flower.
Lyla's rose wasn't perfect,
but she didn't mind—
neither was Lyla.
They were two of a kind.

You see…the rose had a petal
with a big, round, black spot.
Lyla's shell, on the other hand…did not.

In fact…all Lyla's friends
had shells with dots—
some had one
and some had lots.
Lyla the Ladybug's shell had none—
no freckles,
no speckles,
no spots.

Valentine's Day had finally arrived.
Lyla parted the petals and peeked outside.

She spotted a "ten-dotted" ladybug flying nearby.
All the boys liked her.
Lyla didn't understand why.
She wasn't smart or funny.
She wasn't friendly or kind.
She just had lots of dots and…

...a long line of little boy ladybugs flying behind...

...all trying to be her Valentine.

Lyla decided it was time to find out
what this thing called love was really about.

She spied two bees by a hive above,
and decided to see what bees knew about love.

"We love honey!" they buzzed, as they started to dive.
Lyla dove right behind them...straight into the hive!

Lyla liked honey,
that much was true.
But...she didn't love it
like honeybees do.

So...she flew out of the hive...

…just as two butterflies were fluttering by.

She landed on one and held on tight.
She asked about love as they flew toward the light.
"We love sunshine!" they sang out. "It's warm and bright.
See how beautiful our wings look when it hits them just right."

Lyla liked sunshine,
that much was true.
But...she didn't love it
like butterflies do.

So...she flew down to the ground
and landed on top...

…of two tiny ants carrying a big lollipop.

And before she could say a single word,
they answered the question they had already heard.

"We love work!" they called out, marching along.
"We love carrying things to prove that we're strong."

Lyla sat all alone on the cold, hard floor,
more confused about love than she had been before.

Ants love work.

Bees love honey.

Butterflies love the sun.

How could love be
something different to everyone?

Just then…
an imperfect pink petal
drifted down to the floor.
Lyla was sure
she had seen that petal before.

It belonged to her rose.
Her wonderful rose—

the one that she lived in...   ...and took care of,

the one that she shared with, the one that she...LOVED!

You see…

Lyla had known what love was right from the start.
It was how she felt about her rose deep down in her heart.

She raced back to her rose and...

...gave it a hug.
And the hug Lyla gave it was so full of love,
something wonderful happened
to that lovesick little bug.

She got her very first spot!
But…

…the spot Lyla got
wasn't shaped likc a dot.
It was shaped like a heart.
And believe it or not,
that first little spot was only the start!

One by one, more hearts appeared.
All Lyla's friends gathered around her and cheered.

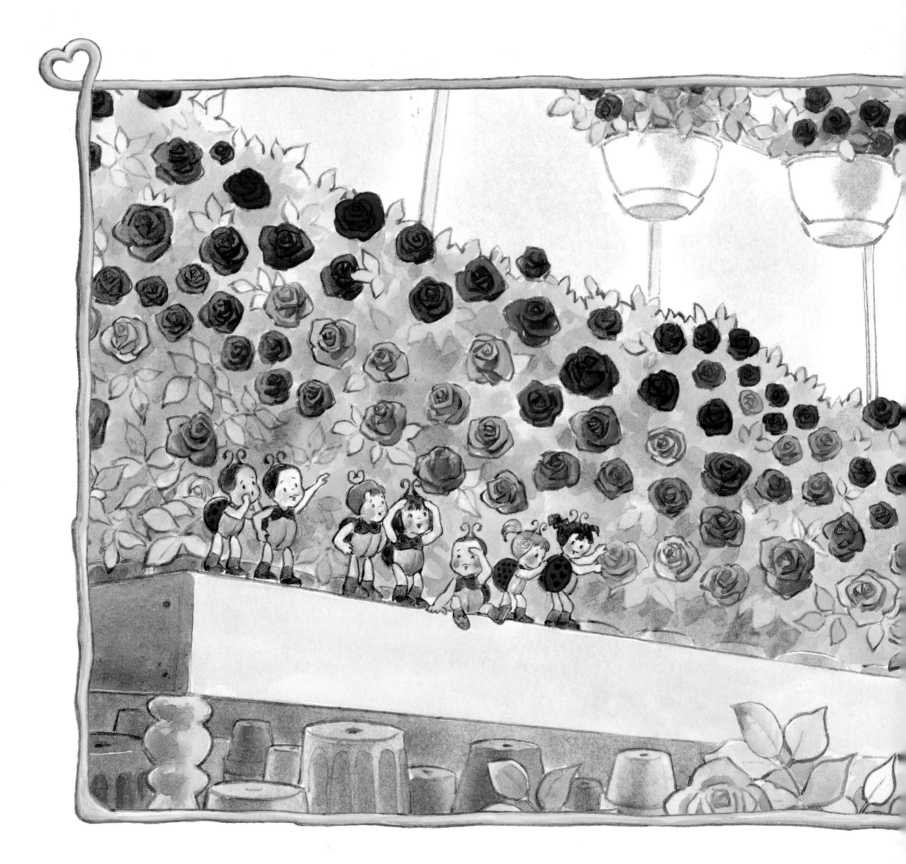

And just as the last heart appeared on her shell,
every rose in the greenhouse bloomed as well.
And each one was beautiful
in its own special way…
just like Lyla the Ladybug, that Valentine's Day.

Lyla learned a lot about love that Valentine's Day.

She learned—
Love is caring.
Love is sharing.
Love can be friendship too.
Love is the greatest gift you can give
and the greatest gift someone can give you.

And that…someone who loves you,
will love you a lot,
whether you have a spot…or not!